MW00913107

AUSSIE BITES

The Way Home

Now that her brother Ben is going

to a different school, Carla has

to walk home with Miranda.

Are Miranda's stories about the

headless cat, the bank-robbers and

the witch really true?

which Aussie Bites have you read?

 THE WAY HOME
Eleanor Nilsson
Illustrated by Betina Ogden

 NO ONE
Eleanor Nilsson
Illustrated by Betina Ogden

 JALEESA THE EMU
Nola Kerr and Susannah Brindle
Illustrated by Craig Charles

 MISS WOLF AND THE PORKERS
Bill Condon
Illustrated by Caroline Magerl

 SERENA AND THE SEA SERPENT
Garth Nix
Illustrated by Stephen Michael King

 EVEN BIGGER WHOPPERS
Moya Simons
Illustrated by Terry Denton

AUSSIE BITES

The Way Home

Eleanor Nilsson

Illustrated by Betina Ogden

Puffin Books

For Ella, whose way home it is. *E.N.*

For my mum. *B.O.*

Puffin Books
Penguin Books Australia Ltd
487 Maroondah Highway, PO Box 257
Ringwood, Victoria 3134, Australia
Penguin Books Ltd
Harmondsworth, Middlesex, England
Penguin Putnam Inc.
375 Hudson Street, New York, New York 10014, USA
Penguin Books Canada Limited
10 Alcorn Avenue, Toronto, Ontario, Canada, M4V 3B2
Penguin Books (N.Z.) Ltd
Cnr Rosedale and Airborne Roads, Albany, Auckland, New Zealand
Penguin Books (South Africa) (Pty) Ltd
5 Watkins Street, Denver Ext 4, 2094, South Africa
Penguin Books India (P) Ltd
11, Community Centre, Panchsheel Park, New Delhi 110 017, India

First published by Penguin Books Australia, 2001

1 3 5 7 9 10 8 6 4 2

Text copyright © Eleanor Nilsson, 2001
Illustrations copyright © Betina Ogden, 2001

Designed by Melissa Fraser, Penguin Design Studio
Series designed by Ruth Grüner
Series editor: Kay Ronai
Typeset in New Century School Book
by Post Pre-press Group, Brisbane, Qld
Printed and bound in Australia by McPherson's Printing Group
Maryborough, Victoria

National Library of Australia
Cataloguing-in-Publication data:

Nilsson, Eleanor.
The way home.
ISBN 0 14 131067 7.

A823.3

www.puffin.com.au

One

'Now that Ben's at another school,
I want you to come home with
Miranda.'

Carla glared at her mother. 'I can
come home by myself. I'm not a baby.'

'Just for the first two weeks,' said
her mother, 'till you get used to not
having your brother around. I've fixed
it up with Miranda's mum.'

Miranda lived next door. She was
a whole year older than Carla.

But Carla was pleased, really, that

she would have someone to come home with. She just wished it didn't have to be Miranda. Miranda already thought she was a wimp.

It wasn't that Carla didn't know how to get home. She had to walk along the main road, go up past the graveyard, and down the little wandery street to the park. It was easy to find her way from there.

But she felt worried about coming through the park by herself. It was fun when she was with Ben, and the best part of the walk. The trees sang with birds. One of the things she always did was to count how many

birds she could see. She liked the
galahs best.

After school on Monday, Carla had to
hang around waiting for Miranda.
She felt itchy with waiting. She hopped
from one leg to the other and swung
her school bag around. Maybe she

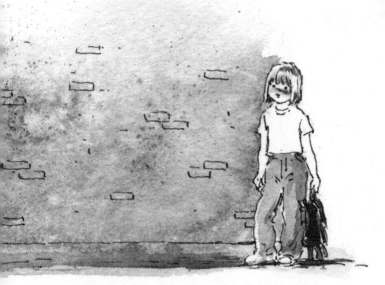

should just go off without her.
Miranda always made her feel stupid
anyway.

Oh, here she was at last. Carla
could see Miranda, tall, confident,
making her way slowly across the
school yard.

'Oh, *there* you are,' said Miranda,

as if Carla was a flea or something, and as if it was Carla who was late.

Carla couldn't help herself. She wanted Miranda to think well of her but knew she was going about it the wrong way. The words came tumbling out. 'I got ten out of ten for my sums today and Miss Egbert said the picture I drew was the best in the class!'

Miranda looked down from her great height. 'Clever little thing, then. Ten out of ten!'

Carla felt even more uncomfortable. Miranda's words were praising her up but the way she said them wasn't.

'How do you think everyone else
feels now about their picture?'
Miranda asked her.

Carla stared at her, puzzled.

'Knowing that it's not the best.'

Then Miranda started humming,
as if she didn't want to be interrupted,
all the way up to the graveyard and

then down again. She only stopped, and looked rather sad, when a dog barked at them from behind a gate.

When they were coming through the park, Carla told her about the galahs. 'See how they're eating the grass seed, and carrying it in their beaks. I think they're so cute. But every time I count them there's only nineteen.'

'You mean they should be in pairs?' Carla nodded.

'That's because she's taken it,' said Miranda, 'that scary woman who lives in the house with the letter-box with flowers painted on it. She's got galah number twenty. She's always catching things and putting them in cages.' Miranda rolled her green eyes. 'People say she's looking for a child to take inside the house.'

Carla shivered. 'To put in a *cage*?'

Miranda nodded. 'Make sure it isn't you. Look, it's that house we're coming to now.'

Carla stared at the house. It looked like any other. It was cream brick with white shutters. The sun shone on it.

Pansies were flowering up the edges
of the driveway.

But what if you could see inside?
The rooms might be dark and filled
with birds, silent in their cages.
In the darkest room of all, its
windows draped in red, a woman
might be waiting – hunched over
an empty silver cage.

Two

On Tuesday, Carla had to wait again at the school gate.

Miranda took even longer to come and was yawning a lot when she reached her. 'Twenty out of ten for your sums today, I bet. What else did you star at?'

'Nothing much,' mumbled Carla.

On the way up to the graveyard Miranda asked her a horrible sum. 'A farmer has 42,000 corellas on his property. He's allowed to kill half

13

of them, but half of the others get injured as well. How many healthy corellas are left?'

'He wouldn't be allowed to shoot the corellas,' said Carla.

Miranda raised an eyebrow.

Carla's voice rose. 'He wouldn't. He *wouldn't.*'

Miranda yawned.

In the park a woman went past
them, out walking her small dog.
Carla noticed that Miranda turned
away and seemed upset.

They were nearly home. They were
coming to a house whose outside
looked dark even on a bright day.

Everything about it was brown. Today, as usual, there were three cars in the drive and one on the road outside.

'I wonder why they have four cars,' said Carla innocently.

She knew her mother was always talking about how expensive even one car was to run.

'Ah,' said Miranda, suddenly coming to life. 'These are the cars of the three men in black. You must have seen them. They've got four cars because they use them in hold-ups. They use the white car to get away in, then they change into that blue one, then the yellow, and last of all . . . the red.'

Carla shivered. She tried to walk faster. 'Why aren't they in jail, then?' she whispered.

Miranda tossed her head. 'They never get caught, of course.'

'And why did you talk about the red car in a funny way?'

'*Did* I?' said Miranda.

'Yes. You sort of stopped as if there was something else.'

'Oh, that.'

Carla waited. She held herself very still.

'I don't really believe this bit,' said Miranda, 'but people say that the last car of all, the red car, isn't filled with petrol at all. It's filled with blood.'

Carla shuddered. She imagined herself standing stiff like a petrol pump while one of the men in black filled up with fuel from her. She could feel all the strength going out of her body. She pictured drops of blood falling on the concrete. A service attendant with a green watering-can washed the drops away.

Three

On Wednesday, Carla's mother
dropped her off at school as usual.

'How are you getting on with
Miranda?' she asked.

'Okay.'

'Don't worry if she's quiet or
perhaps bad-tempered. She's been a
bit down since her dog died. Are you
all right, love? You look pale.'

'I'm okay, Mum,' she said, gulping
a little to keep her breakfast down.
On the way to school they had passed

the service station with its petrol

pumps and green watering-can.

It had made her feel sick.

After school, Miranda turned up

late at the school gate. As usual she

yawned a lot when Carla told her

anything about school and didn't say

much herself. Carla wondered if she

should say something about Miranda's
dog. It was terrible how it had died
like that – run over in the road.
Miranda must feel awful.

They were coming down the little
wandery street that led from the
graveyard and then turned itself left
along the edge of the park. There were

rainbow lorikeets hidden in the tall gums. Carla could tell it was them because their cry sounded sweet.

'See that house there,' said Carla, more for something to say than anything. 'The white one with the greenish windows. I've never seen anyone in that house and there's never a car in the drive or anyone weeding or anything.'

'Oh, Number 46,' said Miranda, in a bored way. 'That's because it's haunted. The last people moved out months ago and nobody's been brave enough to live in it since.'

Carla didn't say anything for

a minute. She knew it was better not to know. But she found herself asking, 'What haunts it?'

Miranda hesitated. 'I don't think we should talk about it.'

'Mir-*and*-a!'

'Oh, all right. People say it's a headless cat.'

Carla tried to imagine it. Then she tried not to. She shuddered.

Four

On Thursday, Carla was surprised
to see Miranda waiting at the school
gate. Miranda was blowing her nose
as if she had a bad cold. Her voice
sounded funny. She walked very fast
on the way home. Carla felt like
a puppy trotting along beside her.

When they got to the cemetery,
Carla said, 'See how that grave on
the end near the road is whiter than
the others?'

'The stone, you mean?'

Carla nodded. 'It's often got real flowers on it, not plastic ones like on the other graves. When I'm dead, I'd rather have no flowers than plastic ones.'

'But will you know?' asked Miranda, raising her eyebrows in

a superior way. 'That's a boy's grave,' Miranda went on. 'He didn't die that long ago. That's why he still gets real flowers. Although people say . . . '

Here followed one of Miranda's long pauses.

'Go on, Miranda.'

'People say he isn't really dead at all.'

'What do you mean?' Carla felt a shiver go all the way down her back.

'He was drowned at the ford, on Winn's Road. It flooded suddenly when he was trying to cross it on his bike. Stupid thing to do. He was swept away and hit his head or something and drowned.'

Miranda looked serious and sad.

'And what happened after?' asked Carla.

Miranda stared at her.

'You said about him not really being dead.'

'Oh, that.'

Carla waited.

'Oh, well, if you want to hear. They say at dusk you can sometimes see him ride his bike. Weeds cling to the pedals and river water streams from his tyres.'

'Oh,' said Carla, in a small voice.

Miranda started walking. 'Come on, I want to get home.'

Five

It was Friday. Carla's mother looked at her anxiously. 'That was Miranda's mum on the phone. Miranda's sick. She can't walk home with you today. Will you be all right?'

Carla tried to smile at her mother. '*Yes*, Mum.'

After school, Carla wasn't in a hurry to go home. The map of her walk had become different. Past the green watering-can, she thought. Past the graveyard with the dead boy on the bike. Past the headless cat, the woman with the empty child's cage, the robbers with three cars in the drive and the dreadful red one on the road outside.

It was the street part of the walk that worried her now, not the park

with its nice galahs. Miranda will probably start on *it* next week, said a little voice inside her head.

Carla was shocked by the voice. Did that mean she didn't believe what Miranda said? Carla thought she believed it and didn't believe it at the same time. Miranda was always so serious. She wasn't the sort of person who made things up.

Carla chatted with Amber and then she played on the swings with Rachel. When Rachel said she had to get home, Carla suddenly noticed that everyone else seemed to have gone. The school was empty. The sky had grown over dark. Carla grabbed her school bag. As she went past the empty spot by the school gate where Miranda should have been, it started to rain.

She walked quickly along the main road as the sky got steadily darker

and the rain heavier. Some of the cars
were even putting on their lights. She
ran past the service station.

She could feel her heart beating
faster and faster as she turned up the
street to the graveyard. She walked
more and more slowly. She could
hardly see for the rain.

As she drew level with the boy's grave, she heard something coming from the direction of the park. Whatever it was, was getting nearer. It was making a strange and ghostly noise. She made herself climb up the bank and she hid, first behind a very

wet bush and then behind a tree.

She was just in time.

A dark figure on a bike pedalled
steadily towards her. Water dripped
from his jacket and river weeds clung
to the pedals and wheels of his bike.
It was the dead boy.

Six

Carla crouched behind her tree, too shocked to cry. She could no longer see or hear the dead boy. The creak of his pedals and the faint hissing noise of his tyres on the wet road had gone. I'll have to move, she told herself. I'm getting so wet and soon it will be quite dark. She licked the rain away from her mouth.

She looked carefully up and down the street. Then she walked out stiffly from behind the tree. Her wet clothes

rubbed on her skin. The bank was
slippery and hard to get down. She
held onto a yellow pigfacey thing and
some of it yanked away in her fingers
as she half fell, out onto the road.

She tried to run on wobbly legs,
round the corner and down the little
wandery street to the park. A dog

barked at her. She followed the street as it turned left. But she was going slower now. Ahead, out of the gathering darkness, she could see the white of the house that no one ever lived in.

She stopped for a moment. Both her

thumbs were firmly crossed. What she would do, she would run really fast past the house and down the path to the park. She got ready. She would count to ten. One . . . two . . . three . . . four . . . five . . . six . . . se . . .

Something flew out in front of her.

She could feel the air change as it went past. It was white, with four legs. Carla choked with horror. It had no head!

She ran and ran across the park. She was sobbing now, great hurting sobs. Trees loomed up black and harsh on either side of her. Bushes scratched at her legs. There were no birds.

Seven

She walked up the street, too tired
to run.

Someone was out at their letter-box.
A grey hood was over their head.

'Hello,' said the someone. 'What are
you doing out in all this rain?'

Carla started to cry.

'Are you lost, dear? Do you want
me to ring your mother? Come on in,
out of the wet.'

Carla stared at the letter-box. It had
marks on it that might be flowers.

It must be the one Miranda had told
her about, belonging to the scary
woman who put things in cages.
In the distance she could hear the
raw screech of a galah.

She backed away and tried to run, but her feet felt heavy and there was a tearing pain in her side.

She thought she could hear a creaking sound behind her. She knew it was the woman, the empty cage swaying in her claw-like hand. But when she turned around, the woman had gone.

Up the street she could see the red car. Tears trickled down her face. She had escaped the dead boy, the headless cat and the cage, but only for this. *'Think,'* she told herself. 'I can always cross the street. That way I'll be further away from it.'

The rain was sheeting down. It was
hard even to walk against it. It was
worse trying to cross the street away
from the shelter of the trees and
houses. She crossed at an angle but
the rain confused her and she wasn't

as far away from the red car as she
had meant to be. She limped past,
trying not to look at it.

But it made no difference, for the
door of the red car was opening.

Eight

Carla tried to scream, but at first the scream was too far inside her to come out. When it came, she couldn't stop. She screamed and screamed.

A very wet boy on a bike pulled up. 'Carla, what's going on?'

The man in black had got out of his car and was looking a bit fed up. 'I was just going to ask her if she was lost or something.'

'It's okay,' said the boy on the bike, 'it's my sister.'

'It's just as well Mum isn't home yet,' said Ben. 'She rang to say she'd be late. You look a mess. Get your wet clothes off and I'll make you some hot chocolate and put a marshmallow in it.'

Carla started to cry again, thinking of the marshmallow.

'No one hurt you or anything?'

Carla shook her head.

She wandered into her bedroom and sat down on the edge of the bed. She tried to pull off her clothes. They were so wet they were sticking to her like an extra skin. She dried herself on the bedspread and reached under

the pillow for her pyjamas. They were
a bit musty and smelt safe. She pulled
them on.

Ben had lit the wood fire and
pulled her blue bean bag in front of it.
She put her hands around the hot
chocolate and then poked at the

marshmallow. It bobbed around on the
surface, getting smaller. She was glad
it was pink.

'Now tell me about it,' said Ben.
'No, don't cry.'

'It was the way home.' Carla's voice
shook. 'At the graveyard, there was

the dead boy on the bike, with river
water dripping from him everywhere
and weeds on his pedals.'

'At the graveyard?' said Ben slowly.
'You mean me?'

'You?'

'I was up there looking for you.'

Carla stared at Ben. He was wearing a black jacket. His pedals *did* creak. 'But what about the river weeds?'

'I rode through the park. I've probably got wet grass on the pedals. They were cutting parts of it this week.' He looked at her, puzzled. 'But why would you think someone on a bike was dead?'

Carla didn't answer him. She was thinking of the second terror, of the white body and the four white legs. 'But there wasn't any head,' she said. 'There wasn't. There *wasn't.*'

'A cat *running* without a head?

It was nearly dark. You must have imagined it.'

'No,' said Carla, with a little wobble in her voice. 'I didn't. I *didn't*.'

She told him about the woman who wanted to put her in a cage like the twentieth galah, and about the

robbers in black who wanted to milk
her for petrol.

Ben looked startled and then
amused and then angry. 'Wait on.
Someone's been filling your head with
stories, haven't they?'

'They're not stories,' said Carla
faintly. 'They're true.'

'Mrs Shaw isn't true. She used
to work at the school. She's nice.
She found that galah hurt and looks
after it.'

'She's *not* nice. She's scary. She is,
she *is*. She wears a grey hood. You
can't even see her face. *She wanted me
to go inside her house.*'

'Out of the *rain*, Carla. Not to *eat* you. And the boys down the road have four cars because they like mending them.'

'Why are their cars all different colours then?' Miranda had made that seem important. It was to do with the hold-ups.

'*I* don't know. Why *shouldn't* they
be different colours? It would be odd
if they were all the same colour,
wouldn't it?'

Carla stared at the speck of pink
that must be her marshmallow. If she
stared at it hard enough, she wouldn't
cry.

Nine

On Saturday, Carla followed Ben around the house.

'Supposing you *were* the dead boy on the bike . . . '

'Hang on,' he said.

'And the lady with the flowery letter-box isn't scary, and the three men in black only mend cars, that still leaves the cat.' There was a note of triumph in her voice.

'You're not still going on about that?'

Carla ignored him. 'I bet you it hasn't got a head.'

Ben sighed. 'All right. How much?'

Carla hesitated. She still had some of her precious birthday money. 'Five dollars,' she said.

'Right. You're on. Let's get it over with. Which house did you say it was?'

They walked past the brown house with its red car out the front, and then the cream house with its flowery letter-box. Mrs Shaw was out weeding in her garden, her head down. Today she looked different – just like anybody else. They went through the park – nineteen galahs – and stopped

in front of the white house with the
greenish glass. Carla thought she
could see someone moving around
inside. Miranda had said no one lived
there.

Ben stared carefully at it, from all
angles. He looked at the garden, at
the trees, he looked in at the windows.

He started to laugh.

'What's funny?' said Carla, who,
even although it was daytime, was
trying to hold onto his hand.

'I think I see what it was.' He
looked at her slyly. 'But maybe you'd
rather keep it.'

'What do you mean?'

'The headless cat. Maybe you'd rather think there is one.'

Carla thought about it. It would make her walk home more exciting.

But she thought she'd had enough of excitement. She would rather count the galahs in the park, see them half hidden in the long grass, pulling out the seeds and waddling around with them. She thought she could see a flash of pink, high up in the gum tree beside her.

'No,' she said at last. 'I wouldn't.'

Ben pointed to a small window at the side. Sitting looking out at them was a cat. It had a snow-white body and white legs.

'But its head is black,' said Ben. 'What a strange-looking cat! Its head wouldn't have shown up in the dark like the rest of it. That'll be five dollars.'

But he was smiling as he said it.

Carla stared at the cat. Was that
all it was? A white cat with a black
head. Why did Ben have to be right
all the time? She wondered if
Miranda had seen the cat at night,
running across the road as she had.
Or was it just something else she'd
made up?

'I'm stupid, aren't I?' she said.

'Not specially. And then that was
what you were expecting to see.
No head, I mean. Not see it, really.'

He looked at her closely. 'I think we
should tell Mum you're old enough

to walk home by yourself. What do
you think?'

Carla nodded her head. She let go
his hand.

Ben winked at her. 'After all, who
needs Miranda?'

From Eleanor Nilsson

My dog and I often take the walk described in *The Way Home*: past the graveyard, through the park, and past the silent houses.

One day, in the park, I counted nineteen galahs. As they always come in pairs, I started wondering about what had happened to the twentieth galah.

That must have given me the seed for the story. The walk itself seems peaceful enough, but it would only take a story or two about the graveyard and the houses to turn it into something sinister . . .

From Betina Ogden

This story reminds me so much of when I was at school. My school was next door to a cemetery and every day, on our way home from school, we would look in and wonder who was there. After that we walked up the laneway and through the golf links (which was forbidden!), and then down the street where I lived.